Copyright © 2011 by Todd H. Goldman. All rights reserved/CIP data is available.
Published in the United States in 2011 by
🍎 Blue Apple Books, 515 Valley Street, Maplewood, NJ 07040
www.blueapplebooks.com
First Edition 03/11
Printed in China

ISBN: 978-1-60905-077-1

10 9 8 7 6 5 4 3 2 1

Bear in PINK Underwear

Todd H. Doodler

🍎 BLUE APPLE BOOKS

Soccer was Bear's all-time favorite sport.
He played with the mighty Red Devils.

And whenever Bear played,
he always wore his lucky underwear.

Today was the big game against the Blue Jays.
The score was tied 0-0. With only thirty seconds left,
it started to rain, really hard.

Skunk passed the ball
to Deer.

Deer kicked the ball
to Big Foot.

Big Foot dove for the ball.

Turtle headed the ball
to Bear.

Bear dribbled the ball, got ready to kick,
and slipped on the wet grass.

Nobody won. Nobody lost.
But everyone was covered in mud,
including Bear and his lucky underwear.

After the game,
Bear was very tired.

He wanted to sleep, but before he could take a nap,
he had to wash his muddy clothes for tomorrow's game.

The next day, the Devils met at the field dressed in their red uniforms.

Bear was wearing his uniform
and his lucky tighty whities.
But wait a minute.
They weren't white.
They were . . .

THIS IS MY LUCKY UNDERWEAR. I HAVE TO WEAR IT!
THEY'RE NOT SO LUCKY ANYMORE— THEY'RE PINK!

Bear ran out onto the field with his head down.
When the Blue Jays saw his shorts, they laughed.

Bear ignored the teasing.
He was busy worrying
about the game.

The game started.
In the first half, Big Foot scored for the Devils.

In the second half, the Jays tied the game.
There was just one minute left on the clock.

Deer flicked the ball to Hedgy.

Hedgy missed and . . .

The ball landed at Bear's feet!
The Jays teased him again.

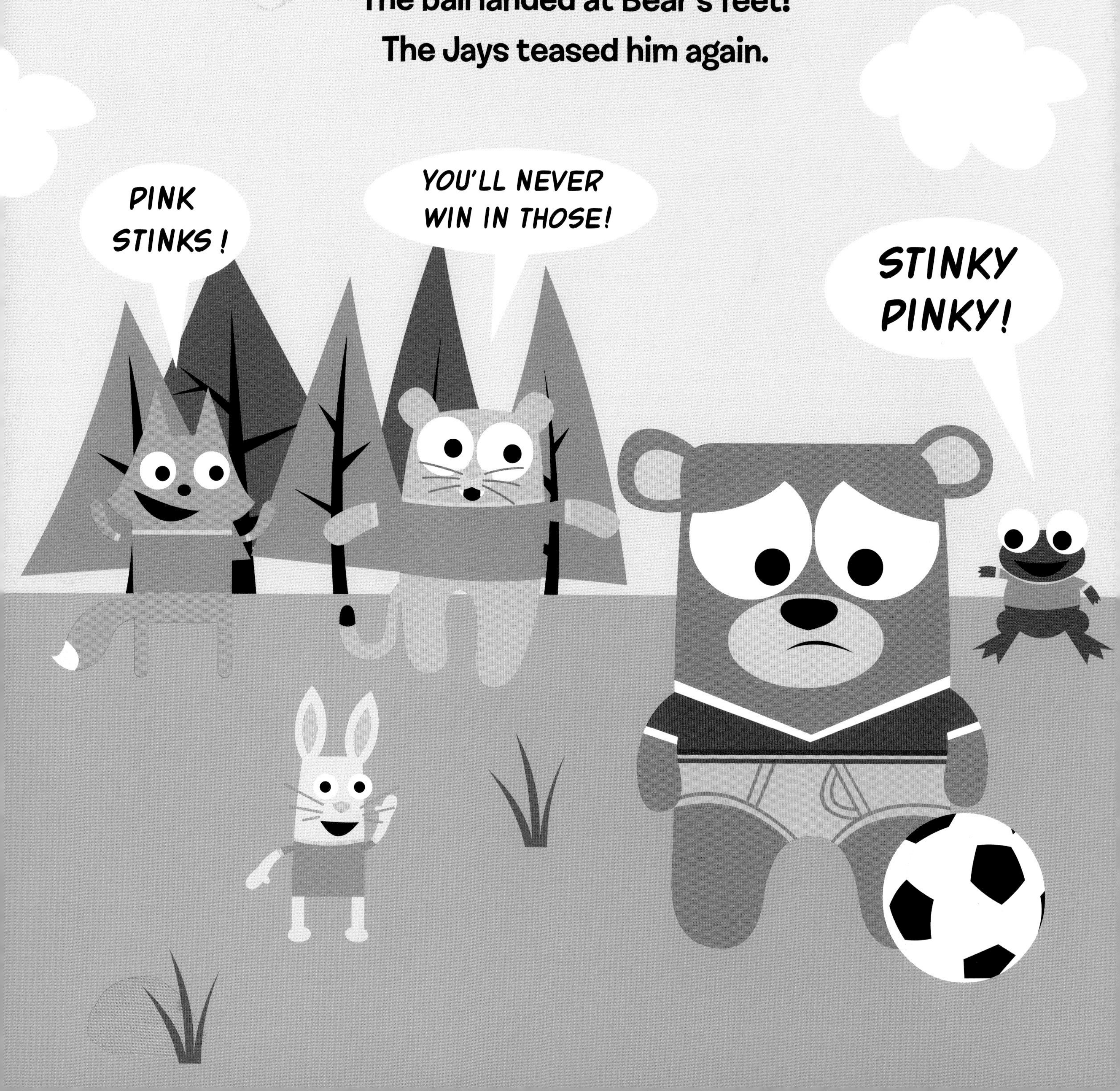

Bear looked at the clock. Thirty seconds to go.

He zigged
to the left.

He zagged
to the right.

He dribbled
back and forth.

He dribbled
up and down.

Bear took a deep breath and closed his eyes.
He kicked the ball with all his might!

The ball flew
through the air—

The Devils won!
Bear scored the winning goal!

Bear's teammates lifted him onto their shoulders
and carried him off the field.

Bear smiled from ear to ear.